THE NIGHT OF THE GIRONDISTS

JACQUES PRESSER was born in Amsterdam in 1899. After taking a degree in Dutch literature and history at the University of Amsterdam, he became a schoolteacher. In 1941 he was recruited by the Germans to teach in the Jewish school they had set up in Holland; but in 1943 his wife was arrested, passing through Westerbork on her way to her death at Sobibor, and Presser went into hiding until the end of the Occupation. After the war he obtained a chair in modern history at the University of Amsterdam. He was author of several works of history, including a monumental study of the destruction of the Dutch Jews under Nazism. While a writer's block was preventing him from completing this great work, he was persuaded to enter a literary competition, and he quickly wrote *The Night of the Girondists*, his hunt for the traces of his lost wife being fresh in his mind. The short narrative was submitted anonymously and was the winning entry. It was published in 1957, and went on to win the Van Hoogt Prize for Creative Literature, awarded by the Dutch Society for Literature. Jacques Presser also wrote a number of detective stories for relaxation. He died in 1970.

Jacques Presser

NIGHT OF THE GIRONDISTS

With a Foreword by
Primo Levi

Translated from the Dutch by
Barrows Mussey

HARVILL
An Imprint of HarperCollins*Publishers*

First published anonymously in Holland in 1957
with the title *De Nacht der Girondijnen*

First published in Great Britain in 1959 by
Frederick Muller with the title *Breaking Point*

This edition first published in 1992 by Harvill
an imprint of HarperCollins Publishers,
77/85 Fulham Palace Road,
Hammersmith, London W6 8JB

9 8 7 6 5 4 3 2 1

The English translation of Primo Levi's Foreword
is by Guido Waldman

A CIP catalogue record for this book
is available from the British Library

ISBN 0 00 271209 1

Photoset in Linotron Garamond No. 3
by Rowland Phototypesetting Ltd, Bury St Edmunds, Suffolk
Printed and bound in Great Britain by
Hartnolls Ltd., Bodmin, Cornwall

The author wishes to point out that, although
this story contains a single borrowing,
plainly apparent to the initiated, none of
the characters is to be identified with any
person still living.

FOREWORD

I stumbled upon this story quite by chance some years ago. I've read it and re-read it and cannot get it out of my mind. Perhaps it is worth looking for the reason: there can be any number of reasons for liking a book, some of them plain for all to see and perfectly rational, others deep-rooted and obscure.

I don't think we are concerned with *how* this story is told. It is told unevenly: some pages are well crafted while others are all too cerebral, too self-conscious and contrived. But, taking each episode, it is very plainly truthful in detail (many other sources bear it out, and Auschwitz inmates have recognized in it the "passengers" who survived the train from Westerbork); so although it may read like a novel, it is stamped with authenticity. But this is not the sole reason for its importance.

This brief work is one of the few that gives literary voice to western European Judaism in a fitting manner. An abundant and splendid literature speaks for eastern Judaism in the Ashkenazi, Yiddish tradition, but the western branch has been deeply rooted in the relevant German, French, Dutch, Italian bourgeois cultures and has contributed to them in full measure; it has only seldom spoken for itself, though. Such strains of Judaism are so conditioned by the Diaspora that they display little unity; meshed as they are with the culture of the host-countries, it is a well-known fact that they do not possess a language of their own. They have been philosophical with the Enlightenment, romantic with the romantics, they have been liberal, socialist, bourgeois, nationalist, and yet, through all the metamorphoses required of them by reason of the time or place, they have retained certain characteristic features, and these are to be found in this book.

Subject as he is to the conflict between the two poles of fidelity and assimilation, the western Jew suffers a chronic identity crisis that explains his equally chronic neurosis, as also his adaptability and sharpness of mind. In the West, the figure of the Jew contented with his Jewishness, the Jew who asks for nothing more than his Jewishness (like the immortal milkman Tevye in Sholem Aleichem) is virtually non-existent.

This is a story about an identity crisis: the protagonist suffers it to such a degree he is quite torn in two. There dwells in him "Jacques", an assimilated Jew who is tied to the Dutch soil if not to the Dutch people; he is a versatile and decadent intellectual, emotionally immature, politically suspect, morally negligible. There also dwells in him "Jacob", who has been retrieved from the past thanks to the efforts and example of Hirsch "the rabbi", and Jacob draws strength from his Hebrew roots which he had hitherto scanted or disowned, and he sacrifices himself in order to rescue from oblivion a Book in which Jacques does not believe. What European Jew has not undergone a similar experience? Or who has never found himself turning in the hour of need for reassurance and moral support to Jewish culture, the very culture which in more halcyon years he tended to regard as passé and irrelevant? Hirsch says as much to Jacques: barbed wire binds, and it binds tight. I am not suggesting that a return to the sources is the only way out, but it is certainly one way.

Another feature that lends weight to this narrative is its objectivity. Certain pages are quite ruthless the way their actual author seems to endorse this "Jewish self-loathing" (another aspect of the identity crisis) that Henriques *père* attributes to his son and wife; here lie the origins of the many anti-Semitic Jews in western Europe, like Weininger, the man cited with admiration by Georg Cohn. To be reminded that at Westerbork a man like Cohn existed and functioned stings like a burn and deserves comment. Such folk have existed before and no doubt still live among us in an embryonic state; in normal conditions they elude recognition (Cohn himself planned to go into banking), but a pitiless persecution promotes their development, brings them out into the light of day and gives them power. It is naïve, absurd and historically inaccurate to maintain that an evil system like Nazism sanctifies its victims: quite the reverse, it leaves them soiled and degraded, it assimilates them, and all the more so to the degree that the victims are at their disposal, virginally innocent of any political or moral constructs. Cohn is execrable, of course, a monster who needs to be punished, but his crime simply reflects a different crime, far more serious and widespread.

It is no coincidence that in the last few years books have been published like H. Langbein's *Menschen in Auschwitz* and Gitta Sereny's *Into That Darkness*. There are enough signs to indicate that the time has come to explore the space that divides the victims from their executioners, and to go about it with considerably more delicacy and clearsightedness than has been evident, for instance, in certain well-known recent films. It would take a Manichean to argue that such a space is empty. Empty it is not: it is studded with sordid, deplorable or pathetic creatures (occasionally the three at once) and it is vital to recognize them if we hope to understand the human race, if we hope to be able to protect our inner selves should a similar trial ever recur.

Evil exists in contagious form: the man who lacks humanity deprives others of theirs, every crime spreads, propagates itself, corrupts other people's consciences and surrounds itself with accomplices seduced from the opposite camp by means of terror or (as in Suasso's case) enticements. A typical feature of criminal systems like Nazism is that they debilitate and cloud our judgment. The man who betrays under torture, is he guilty? Or the one who kills in order to save his own skin? Or the soldier on the Russian front who cannot desert? Where shall we draw the line in the empty space I just mentioned, to segregate the bad from the weak? Is Cohn to be held to account?

Well, the drift of the book is that Cohn is indeed

accountable. His remark about the "leaking vessel" is disingenuous; so is his claim (we've heard it enough times before!) that "if I didn't do it, someone else would who's even worse than I am." A stand *has* to be made, it always can be, in every case, if only by following in the steps of Miss Wolfson. If you don't make a stand (and you must do it from the word go, you must keep your hands well clear of the mechanism), you eventually yield to the temptation to change sides; at best, your resulting gratification will be unreliable and your safety itself destructive.

Cohn is guilty but with an attenuating factor. The prevailing conscience that will not yield to violence but resists it belongs to today: it is *post facto*, it did not then exist. The imperative of resistance matured with the Resistance and with the global tragedy of the Second World War; prior to that, it was the precious heritage of the few. Even today it does not belong to everyone, but today those who wish to understand may do so, and I think this book can help them.

One may like a book or a person but that does not mean that one is blind to its or his faults. This book has its share, maybe it has serious faults. The style is unsettled, wavering between the emotional and the flippant. Presser often leaves the impression that he is not immune from the literary flights of his *alter ego* Henriques, with a weakness for reciting quotations even at death's door. Occasionally he will confront a harrowing situation with complacency where a restrained silence would have been more appropriate.

A debatable book, then, maybe a scandalous one; but it is good that scandals should come, for they provoke discussion and make for inner clarity.

PRIMO LEVI

THE NIGHT OF THE GIRONDISTS

HOMO HOMINI HOMO

I'LL TRY JUST ONCE MORE. Perhaps it won't work, either, and the figures won't add up, any more than they would a fortnight ago, any more than last week. Twice now I have torn up the precious scrap of paper, but this is my last chance; delaying, putting off is impossible now that I myself am in the punitive barracks, with full assurance of "rolling off eastward", to use a prize specimen from Cohn's vocabulary. If there is no intervening convoy – "Organization means improvisation, Suasso!" – I may have six or seven days left, and the only question is whether my figures will add up well enough to give an answer, right or wrong, but anyhow the answer that I have twice failed to get, neither right nor wrong.

Right or wrong, neither right nor wrong. The jingling syllables are a nuisance. What I probably ought to do above all is to lay down a board in front of me with the words, *I am not mad.* I certainly can't go beyond that. I honestly feel that I am in my right mind, and the only thing that disturbs me is my need to keep saying so. Not mad, not crazy, not insane. If I could just assume the opposite, everything would be much simpler, and I might just drop this scribbling altogether. But I have to cling to the fact of my sanity, and one motive force of the machine is . . .

Stop. Motive force, motive force, motive force. Penal camp, turnip soup, fiery glare. Oh, those damned, pounding dactyls, the *bangety* of those words that pretend to communicate some significance, some meaning to us. It keeps resounding, not loud but insistently: Bangety. Just the same as the other times: a word causing a short circuit.

And it's precisely that queer experience, a thousand years away, a week before the war, May 1, 1940 (1940 – I could rub my eyes out!), when I drove Mother's little DKW to pot; bangety went the gearbox, and there I stood. Driving force, driving force. Words themselves threaten to go on strike, and yet I have to build this account out of words; I can't just babble senselessly, whump, whish, plop, glurp. I don't know, possibly that is the only language that would give an adequate reflection of the situation ("adequate," now, that's three from Cohn's stock: haven't I got rid of him yet?). If I write correct grammar and an educated style, what I'm going to tell will certainly seem like even greater nonsense, completely without meaning.

All right, let's start over again. The DKW finally ran again, too. I want something; all right. So I have a driving force. Quiet, damn it, driving force. To undertake something impossible, something that simply can't be done; that's what my reason says, the servant faced with the dirty job. Let's get on with it. Possibly "man in his dark urge" – I was just waiting

4

for that quotation from Goethe; with my kind, it always turns up sooner or later.

Goethe. Yes, Goethe, Heine, again and yet again Heine, Novalis, Hölderlin, every one of them was in Father's room. And Mörike. Make sure I don't forget Schiller, another of those quotation-factories. And Platen – another anti-Semite like your mother and you, Father joked once. But without your Jewish self-hatred that makes your mother keep running after that fellow, what's his name again? (Father gave a very poor imitation of Freud, because the name of Bolland was quite ready to his tongue). The Germans are right when they call us *"meshuggene* Portuguese", with people like you – father was forgetting Uncle Felix Osorio de Castro, who (I swear it) arrived in Westerbork and promptly asked me in an injured tone for a room with bath. No, he said, better Goethe, he . . .

Over Father's desk, just the thing for a humanist like him, hung a motto in Greek: Know thyself. That was his pride, that and his fine goatee, because he really was a little vain. The goatee is the last thing I ever saw of him; it was sticking up as he lay on the pavement, and his arms and legs foolishly flung out. The street was blacked out, of course, but so full of blue-white moonlight that the silly little object cast a small shadow of its own, next to the black pool of blood. They had come to fetch Mother and him, and he had been firmly resolved to go along quietly, because nothing could happen to him as a Portuguese: after all, hadn't he a stamp? He must have fled over the roofs; they fired in the air, not at him, they said. As for the other links, what difference would it make if I knew them? Know thyself . . . Mother was already in the Jewish Theatre, the front gate to our camp, but I, his own son, happening to be busy about a job two or three streets beyond, was fetched: the goatee in the moonlight. Remember it, says Jacob. Your father lay there, probably half an hour, just like that. Don't only think of the beard, but of the pool of blood, too. Don't forget, don't forget.

Had I forgotten after all? Yes, no; yes, no. After all, that was then; now it won't leave my memory; I recall exactly how it was. Rereading the last paragraph, I can say: this, this is exactly how it was. Poe would have told it differently, but, once again: *this is how it was.* I underline the words twice, not just for myself; I am also addressing a fellow reader who is looking over my shoulder. Who it is I don't know. When this document is smuggled out of the camp according to my will, some day there will be somebody or other. Not a Jew, I imagine. So much the better. Let him say, What rot. Let him say, The man's having a fit. But he mustn't say, Grand Guignol. And above all, not, He's imagining it. Let him believe. Let him assume that my eyes saw this, my ears heard it, my hand brushed gently over Father's. Even unbelievers sometimes don't dare walk under a ladder – knock wood. All right, raise your right hand: I, Jacques Suasso Henriques, born February 24, 1916, swear: this is the whole truth, unadorned, unexaggerated. And this oath holds good, inviolable, for all that follows, word by word and letter by letter.

The school. I suppose I shall have to begin there. That pedagogical and ethnic travesty, the Jewish High School, the ghetto school allowed by the Germans. With Jewish teachers, Jewish children; with orthodox and freethinkers, with Zionists and assimilationists (like me; behind my back it was "ass-imilationists"), with an assortment of the baptized, with circumcised and uncircumcised, with Dutch, stateless, Turkish, Romanian children, and − just as here at the camp − one single little citizen of Honduras. This last national- ity was and is pretty much a vogue, but when the father of the schoolgirl Leah Cohn went to the German Zentralstelle to get the sheltering rubber stamp, he suffered the misfortune of being completely unable to remember the capital of his distant fatherland, and so the whole family has for some time been in Auschwitz, the capital of Poland.

We were talking about the school. In September, 1942, with the new school year, suddenly there were both Georg Cohn in Class 5A and Ninon de Vries in 6B. The last-named I can treat briefly at this stage of my story. Luckily I needn't act literary, and so I can say straight out: This was the most divine young girl I have ever seen among the daughters of the Jewish race (why don't you say *our* race? Jacob jeers), and in a couple of weeks I realized I was completely crazy about her. The name Ninon suited her wonderfully; she was the daughter of an Amsterdam diamond merchant who had lived in Paris: there was something roguish, some- thing faintly tingling about it − if I had not had to carry her on to the train myself, I might never have known her real first name, the one on her identification papers – Sadie, plain Sadie, like a Jewish joke. Not that it bothered me much then any more; and besides, anyone that goes by the name of Jacques . . . But above a certain level it is probably easier to bear an exotic name like that, and the old gentleman, Nathan de Vries, the "big man", was in fact fabulously rich; she may have picked up from him the notion she brought to school about "*nebbish* teachers", barely good enough to prepare sons and daughters like her for the university. She let us feel it, and in particular made it plain to the dull dog who was so infatuated with her. And then all at once she was gone from the school. Here, in a couple of dozen words, I have thrown away the material for a full-length novel, but I am in a hurry, and I shall have to come back to her anyway.

Besides, her departure from school, taken all in all, was only one of the causes (motive forces – stop it! – motive forces) of my own transition from then to now, from there to here. Because, miserable though I was about it, my experience with Georg counted at least as much, even though I took much less notice of it then, and certainly less of his unhappy disposition. My first true meeting with Georg took place one October afternoon a couple of days after the great raid for the labour camps. I had his class, 5A, for the last hour of the school day, and while the other children were leaving, he visibly hesitated; when we were alone, he shut the door, came toward me with his hand in his inside pocket, and suddenly showed me a stack of bank notes. I can still see his smiling young face (he was just seventeen, and girlishly good-looking), and particularly the hand that carried the money slowly in a smooth curve past my eyes. "Three thousand, nine hundred and forty guilders," he said, as it were, airily. "That's close enough to four thousand. Just picked it up after lunch. Black market."

Was he telling the truth? Now I believe he was; at the time I was much more doubtful. Normal and abnormal had not yet started changing places so plainly as they have since. Later he showed me much more, sometimes accompanied by an explanation not dreamt of in my philosophy. Naturally he wanted to attract my attention, and later I sometimes asked myself whether he was not offering me the money, or at least hoping to invoke some incautious reaction on my part. All this came later, when I knew more about him and understood him better.

This went on for a couple of months. At least once a week he would go through the same performance: tête-à-tête, his outstretched hand full of money. I asked him once more where it came from, but the answer was invariable: "Black market, sir." Sometimes the amount was less, often more; once he remarked with an odd sneer that he had just about matched this year in the Jewish chronology, something around six thousand guilders. The first week after the Christmas holidays — I had only had her in class once after the vacation — Ninon, as aforesaid, suddenly vanished. Georg probably knew, or at least suspected, something of what it meant to me, because that sort of child is usually on to a teacher in love before he realizes it himself — what drivel all this scribbling is, but I've got to work myself out of it. In any case, just then came the invitation to have lunch with him – with *him*, take note, for his father (as I and all the Jews in Holland from the Dollart to the West Scheldt well knew) was uncrowned king of Westerbork; his mother was 1. dead, 2. gone, 3. divorced, 4. living with a Dutch professor (subsequent Westerbork slander; please cross out what does not apply). I said yes without much hesitation, and went of a Wednesday in the second week of January to his house in Lairesse Street. That there were great mansions there I knew, but I had not expected anything so enormous as this. Georg, who opened the door for me himself, led the way through a gigantic hall and then through a series of rooms full of huge furniture to a garden room where a table was set for two. I can't help it if this sounds like a fairy tale, particularly in the year 1943, but I am truly not suffering from familiar camp culinary fantasies when I report the indescribable things that were there after three years of war: caviar, if you please, lobster, cold chicken, all kinds of delicate and spicy titbits, all on spotless linen, among gleaming silver and sparkling glass; the coffee, which he deftly poured out himself, had no trace of any adulterant, the cigar was perfection. I confess that I simply had not the courage then, in the face of this shattering reality, to ask where it all came from; at the time, no doubt, I still translated it too largely into purchase prices, and only afterward did I take account of the incredible tightropewalking of this seventeen-year-old lad, this schoolboy, who had organized all this in the insanely huge building where he lived (or so it appeared, though I don't dare assert it for a fact) all by himself.

I can still see him standing beside a monster seventeenth-century panelled cabinet, against the background of heavy red velvet portières, a cigarette carelessly between his fingers, as he abruptly turned the conversation to a completely personal note: "Mr Henriques – or must I say Suasso Henriques? No? Good, Mr Henriques, may I ask you something? What do you really think about Jewry? About the Jews? Just generally?"

"Well, now, Georg, what do I think about the Jews? What do you mean?"

"Well, after all, we're both *Volljuden*, full-blooded Jews, aren't we? With two parents, four grandparents . . . Do you know, once in camp when I had nothing to do I multiplied two to the fourth power. Like that story about the chessboard, you remember. A twenty-digit figure, nothing but Jewish ancestors. Have you that many yourself?"

"Probably. We Portuguese have even more than you."

"So much the worse," he observed. "Don't be startled. I *hate* the Jews. And *Jewry*. It's a disaster. It's more than a disaster. It's a plague."

I can still see that fierce face and the eyes.

"Luckily you aren't shocked. I didn't think you would be, or I'd have held my tongue. Have you read Weininger? No? *Sex and Character*, a hell of a book. Something like that ought to be required reading for every Jew, and they should stop the Talmud or whatever that flapdoodle is called. Weininger, now. They say I'm a lot like him. Look for yourself."

He picked up and opened a book that lay on the piano. Sure enough, like as two peas, although I did not yet understand the depths of the similarity. He was obviously taken with my frank agreement, slammed the book shut, and suddenly jumped to another subject.

"I've talked to Dad about you."

"About me?"

"About you. After all, you know very well what confronts the Jews. Oh, yes, I know – of course you're on the Portuguese list. No doubt because some Henriques lived in Oporto in 1703. Well, much good may it do you. Every list blows up, as they say at Westerbork; no official stamp is ever sure. It's all a fake and a fraud, the whole lot. Before summer of 1943 they'll clear out the whole of Amsterdam. Are you going underground?"

"I don't know."

"It's getting to be time. You'd laugh yourself sick, a fellow like Mr Acohen, saying to me, 'My lad, if you keep letting your physics slide, you'll find yourself taking a make-up exam from me during the vacation.' During the vacation! And Miss Wolfson, she says I've got to tutor in algebra. Make-ups and tutoring. What idiots people are!" He laughed, but was immediately grave again.

"If you're planning to do anything, you'd better do it soon – either go underground now, do you hear, *now*, or . . ."

"Or?"

"Or look for a ninety-nine per cent safe spot. There's no such thing as a hundred, but Dad can probably get you something with that one per cent discount."

"And where do I find this ninety-nine per cent?"

"Just one place in Holland. At Westerbork. No, don't laugh; Dad said so himself, and he doesn't joke. I'll be going there myself in a couple of months, when I reach the danger zone. But you'll be in that before I am; you feel that, don't you?"

"But what am I to do at Westerbork?"

"Exactly. That's the point. Here it is: take the job of jobs, and by that I mean Dad's Disposition Service, the DS. No matter who else has to go, they'll leave by the last train; that's obvious. But there's another reason why you can very well get in there." He hesitated a moment. "Look, I'm about to say something you'll probably think is crazy; I've felt all along that this was no ordinary conversation between teacher and pupil, but let's get on with it. I've been thinking about it a long time, but this morning during the lesson it occurred to me again."

"You're making me quite curious."

"All right, it was during that story about the last night of the Girondists. That was good, you know; I suppose you realize that you're a hell of a fine storyteller? We all think so. And you had it well prepared; one can always tell about that. You were in fine form: I think you said it was by some Frenchman or Englishman; damn, I've forgotten the names. I suppose I should brush up my history!"

I laughed. "Lamartine and a bit of Carlyle."

"All right. But do you remember my asking if it had all really happened just so about the Girondists? Naturally I didn't say so, but it struck me like a novel, a tall story. Yes, really. But you said yes, it really happened. And I thought again, the man just has no idea. No idea of what goes on. I've noticed that more than once before. You thought it was wonderful, you — please don't be angry — well, you wallowed in it. And in that case you have to have seen something or other of the sort. At Westerbork, where I was during the holidays, with Dad. At Christmas. Yes, really, I stayed there. I got a ride in a German army truck, wearing my star. Dad always takes care of that. We had a tremendous talk there, and I told him all about you. And do you know what he said? You really won't be angry? He said, well, he said, Send him here. I'll make a man of him. But tell him to hurry."

I AM GETTING TIRED. Here I sit in the punitive barracks at Westerbork, and I want to know, I *must* know how it happened; I want to add up my figures. How did I get here? The business with Ninon? The talk with Georg? Undoubtedly it was also the atmosphere at school, with all the frantic family men among my colleagues, who could barely be kept going with their daily shots of consolation ("If you don't believe the war will be over next month, you're no good"). Undoubtedly also the children with their stars, the dirty-yellow gobs of spit that they dared not even leave off their hired costumes in a play about the Stastok family in our school gymnasium, for fear of possible informers – Mietje with the popeyes and Mr van Naslaan with six-pointed spots of slime on their chests. And there was the job itself: I was probably too young and too immature for it; I remember, in a class with a lot of girls, talking about this Directoire, which is also the Dutch expression for panties, how I kept avoiding the word, to the great delight of the young demons, who of course clapped mercilessly when the bell rang. What else? After all, I can't recite my entire life for the benefit of my later reader. There was Mother, turned down as a member of the Dutch Nazi Party, in spite of her openly professed "concept" in favour of "the new Germany"; Mother, who had joined the Remonstrants because she felt it was such a "nice church" – oh, I must have been the typical assimilationist child, "emancipated" enough to eat ham, and merely getting more presents than usual on his "thirteenth birthday" because of Father's faintly surviving sentiment for the old days, even two umbrellas from old, old friends who still remembered Grandfather as a mendicant *schnorrer* ("schnorrero," Father said derisively). Never mind, never mind. The manhunts, the stars, the regulations, the humiliations – wasn't all that enough by itself? How I hated – and envied – the Germans, who had marched in here with such supreme self-assurance; how I hated, even more profoundly, all the bewildered, utterly terrified Jews who had fluttered to Ijmuiden at the capitulation – a small advance guard of that blasted people, fleeing through the centuries, never permanently taking root, to whom I belonged without ever having wished it; how I despised our next-door neighbour, who, at the news of the capitulation, had indeed given death to his wife and little daughters, but had stopped short of himself, had been too weak for nonbeing, the very best of all! I had belonged to the Boy Scouts, had ridden horseback, at the university had joined the student fraternity (only to discover, rather regretfully, how little anti-Semitic it was, taken all in all), and had been too weak myself to get into one of the many noisy fascist organizations, just as, heaven knows why, I had obstinately refused to follow Mother's example and accept baptism. Perhaps after all because of Father, too helpless, with his too many books and his unavailing flight into a meaningless Greek dictum.

I give up; I will only tell about my last morning at school. The History of the Fatherland, in Class 2A; don't laugh: the History of the Fatherland. The eighteenth century in 2A, the class that had started in September with thirty children, of whom fourteen remained. I'll just put down, I simply can't help it, that I actually turned in a list of absentees, of *absentees*. I feel like screaming, like kicking a couple of tables and benches to pieces here; I dutifully reported *absentees* to the office, for pupils will not absent themselves without notice, and these children had given no notice, or their parents hadn't – damn!

It was Selma Katan's turn; I stood ready with the book. Teacher all over. "And Selma" (the amiably pedagogic note), "where was the Princess of Orange stopped?"

No reply. So Selma did not know where the Princess was stopped, after all a not unimportant fact listed on page 24 of the *Concise History of the Netherlands*, assigned as homework last time.

"Near Goejanverwelle Lock," I said, now reproachfully pedagogical. "Oh, so you don't know. And in what year?"

Then something struck me. Betsy van Witsen, the ambitious little eager beaver, always trying to get the better of the rather soft Selma, was looking. Not waving her hand with the answer, not with her black head

17

thrust forward as usual. She simply looked, and when I turned to her inquiringly, she said: "Her mother's been taken."

"Her mother?"

"Yes, sir. Selma's mother. Race pollution, they say."

And then Selma herself, struggling against tears: "And she'd had herself sterilized, because they said . . ." Then she was crying. This is true; I could repeat it at the Last Judgment: this is what a thirteen-year-old girl said, those very words, in Class 2A of the so-called Jewish High School.

What next? I put down my book, and let the children "work individually for the rest of the period," the classic phrase of teachers who don't feel like keeping going. My pupil Selma Katan had not known about the Goejanverwelle Lock, indeed had probably left the whole *Concise History* to its own devices, and when I learned the reason for this ignorance, I took the first step, because of that basically fatuous trifle, on my way to this camp, and thence to these barracks. So I might say that I, too, was stopped at the above-mentioned lock, just like the Princess; I walked out of school without saying goodbye to anyone, and foolishly dumped the contents of my bag, the *Concise* and other equally admirable histories, from the High Bridge into the Inner Amstel, and left the students to work individually. I believe they were well pleased, since the following period they had an algebra test, and Miss Wolfson was certainly no one to trifle with.

OF COHN I KNEW, at the moment, only what the Amsterdam Jews were saying about him and the little that his son Georg had added. From him, at least, I had learned that his name was Siegfried Israel, Siegfried, like every German before Hitler, the obligatory Israel like every German Jew under Hitler; I had actually seen it on the calling card that Georg had rather proudly shown me: *Siegfried Israel Cohn, temporary address Westerbork, Holland* – neat, very neat indeed. Of the first few days I can only say that he overpowered me; that's the word for it. To begin with, his gigantic figure, with his boots, his riding breeches, the yellow leather jacket where you could hardly make out the star at all, the tanned brown face with Nordic blue eyes: the Blond Beast. His gruff voice: at last one Jew that really knew how to give orders. His whole position. If I had not known, I would instantly have discovered it from the way I was brought to him: he was obviously among the most exalted of the self-appointed VIPs. (I was one myself for a while.) He had a cottage of his own next to "Goyville" (the building for the baptized inmates), and I was conducted, ahead of anyone else, through a waiting room, where even then, overcome as I was by first impressions, I noticed an unusually large number of women, nearly all young.

He greeted me quietly, not unamiably, but with a clear touch of condescension; for his part, he addressed me familiarly from the start, and called me, as he always did thereafter, Suasso, not Henriques as everyone else did, while my friends naturally addressed me as Jacques, and Father was the only one who sometimes said "Jake" (I was named after Grandfather). Certainly, his son Georg had spoken and written about me at length, and he should know: "Yes, Suasso, my son is a genius." This quite seriously; from later conversations I can confirm it: an unshakable dogma.

"But now let's get down to brass tacks, Suasso: Auschwitz. The name says something to you, I suspect."

"Naturally, sir."

"Good. I suppose you know the fable of the Lion's Den. I've never yet seen a sign of anyone coming back from Auschwitz. In Amsterdam they say they have letters from there. Nonsense. Last week somebody from here boarded the train with an assortment of music books in his knapsack. He thought a house with garden and built-in refrigerator plus Bechstein grand piano were waiting there specially for him and his five children."

I laughed. He remained serious.

"No, Suasso, no. I don't know anything, not to say *know*. Even Schaufinger doesn't know anything, and after all, he's the camp commandant. Adelphi, you know, at the Central Office in Amsterdam, even he hasn't any idea. Well, they're all ordinary policemen the moment they hand over their prisoners, they're through and don't ask any more questions, right? Rauter, at The Hague, is supposed to know more about it, but he says nothing. Not good, if you ask me. Anyhow, subject to contrary information, I assume it's definitely unhealthy for us out there. So I'm just staying here as long as I can, and I assume you'll follow my good example."

"Gladly, sir."

"Good, Suasso, good. But in that case you, like me, fall under the first law of this camp: them or me. The only question is, whom do we mean by them? And the miserable part of it is that only in the long run do we mean the Germans; in the short run it's the Jews. Get it?"

"The Jews?"

"The Jews. Every week Schaufinger gives me the number that go on the train to Auschwitz. It's wired to him every week from The Hague; I suspect, but don't know for sure, that The Hague gets it from Berlin. It's my job to supply the Jews, here and now. Every Monday noon I hear how many, and then we, a couple of supervisors and I, make up the lists. The lists of Jews that will go on Tuesday morning to labour service, as it is officially called."

"To Auschwitz."

"Sure enough, to Auschwitz. Beyond that they proceed horizontally or vertically — vertically, if that's what you want to believe. Another thing: nobody really knows anything, not to say know. But over there they've put a man in charge who has screamed out in a thousand speeches that he's going to exterminate us, and at all the thousand harangues his helpers – what am I saying, the whole German people – have bellowed *Sieg heil!* Yes, yes, never mind, I know: not everybody. But still enough to carry out the plan now that he's been this long in power. Not a soul dreams of balking . . ."

I plucked up courage: "You don't balk yourself, Mr Cohn."

"True enough, I don't balk either. Come, Suasso, try to understand me and don't talk so silly. What do you expect? What can I do, what can we do here? A ship with a thousand passengers has sprung a leak, and not a soul answers our SOS. And there's room in the lifeboats for fifty. Your turn. Well?"

I said nothing.

"But I understand you all right. Fine, suppose I balk. What do you think will happen then? Then next Tuesday I'll be in the train, and Schwarz becomes Central Supervisor, and does the same thing I'm doing. And as soon as he balks, Rosenfeld. And after him, Goldstein or Sacher. As long as there are Jews here, they'll keep finding somebody who is ready if necessary to put his father and mother . . ."

"His father and mother?"

"Yes, Suasso, his own father and mother – are you listening? – on the train. Please remember what I'm about to say. According to everything Georg has written, you'll be my adjutant here. What that is doesn't matter as long as you have an arm-band on, and keep

22

close to me. But that isn't enough. You'll have to grow hard as iron, hard as concrete. Otherwise you're no use, and I won't be able to save you. Camp Law Number 2: the soft or the half-soft go aboard the train. Even I can't do a thing about it. In Amsterdam they think I can do anything here, don't they?"

I nodded.

"Nonsense again. They think Schaufinger is a sort of *Roi fainéant*, and that Cohn's his major-domo. If it were only true. There's a little something to it, just a little. I do the dirty work – there isn't any other work here. Schaufinger lets me alone as long as things here run quietly, without friction and that sort of thing. My will is law as long as I don't will differently from him. The most negligible Aryan here is more powerful than the greatest Jew. Just look at the Dutch constabulary. Fine fellows, for that matter; there's just one of them you have to watch out for, the one they call Red Hein, because he's a wrong one; he's the only one. Schaufinger isn't bad either, for a camp commandant, and I've seen my share. Schaufinger is what you might call tolerable; he at least liquidates us punctiliously. You can just take me as the Jew Süss of the outfit."

"At least you say it yourself, sir."

"Naturally, my boy. Otherwise I'd be long gone, and Georg too. In my camp career I've learned a few things about what I may conscientiously call the realities of life. From '33 on. Yes, man, that makes a definite change in life, take it from me. Did you see the skirts in the waiting room? *Homo sum*, that means. Know what Napoleon yelled to his Mameluke when

23

the spirit moved him? No? And you're supposed to be a historian, God help us. Well, he yelled, '*Roustan, une femme!*' Did you think I could stand this life without shouting out tomorrow or the day after or sometime, '*Suasso, une femme*'? I won't say nine, but I can get six out of ten for nothing if I just keep them off the train. What else could they offer here? The men, money; women . . ."

"And then are they safe? After all, you said . . ."

"All right, Suasso. They're safe, for a week. A week of seven whole days. We all live by the week here; it starts Tuesday morning and ends Tuesday morning: the minute the train pulls out. I said that before, didn't I? Certainly, my boy, I know as well as you do that it isn't pretty, but either they get me or I get them. It's my doing, they say. But to that I answer, 'All right, but not my doing alone. Did I invent Westerbork? Your Dutch government did that.'"

"For quite the opposite purpose, though."

"Right. But just let me say this: you try spending a few years with evil purposes in German camps, and with good purposes in a Dutch camp, and see what survives of your humanity and morality. You're the only Dutchman I'll do anything for, thanks to my boy. Last week a lady from your Apollolaan came to me. That's your smart neighbourhood, isn't it? All right. She wanted different work, loftier work, intellectual, God knows what. Really too genteel – she didn't want to clean latrines. I refused, and said perfectly quietly, 'No, ma'am, as long as we maintain a digestive system, you'll do that job.' And then, you know, the woman

24

let me have it: I was a dirty Boche, and when the war was over she'd settle with me."

"So what did you say?"

"Say? My lad, I can plainly see you don't know Cohn yet. I didn't say anything, I did something. I reported the 'dirty Boche' directly to Schaufinger, and two days later she and her husband, her old mother and her three daughters of seventeen, fifteen, and twelve – you should have seen those girls, Suasso, they were splendid, real angels! – well, she went aboard the cattle car to Auschwitz. She can spend her time there thinking up something for me, for after the war. And be doing intellectual work in the meantime."

I could not suppress a little shudder. He noticed, and went on: "Damn it, Suasso, for the third and thousandth time, harden yourself. What do you expect, anyway? I will stay alive, really not for myself, because after ten years of camp and things, I've had about all there is. I'm only doing it for that boy of mine – he's a genius, I told you, he's an artist at living, a Rimbaud, a Dorian Gray. You've got to understand. If I have to, I'll pull that boy clean through the flames of hell. I will be top man, if I have to unveil statues or launch ships out here on this moor; I'll keep my face straight, I don't care what. Do as I do, Suasso, do as I do. You and I hope to see the day when we jointly string up Schaufinger on the gallows. But there's only one way to get there, and I've shown you what it is. Well, what do you say to that?"

"I'll do my best, sir."

"Good, Suasso, agreed. Remember, you don't need

to work here for nothing. You have one of the safest jobs there is here, that's one point. And as I promised Georg, I'll make a man of you; that's the second point. And furthermore" (he grinned) "what I can't use from the waiting room is at your disposal. Don't look so blank, Suasso. Do you suppose I feel like joking? You know, the rate is one week's postponement. That's what I call the barter system – right? Westerbork seigniory! Would you believe I'd studied economics once myself, that I wanted to be a banker and make something of myself? No, you can't believe that, can you? But it's true. Only . . . Ten years of camps – and then some. Oh, well. You'll do it, will you?"

I stuck out my hand, and he shook it vigorously. The pact with the Devil was sealed.

THE PACT WITH THE DEVIL. I withdraw
the expression; it is not genuine, it is literature. I was
no Faust, he was no Mephisto, and as for Gretchen
. . . He was no Mephisto, certainly not, but he was a
German, who reminded me from the first of Tucholsky's quip: he bought a dog whip and a small dog to
go with it. He actually carried a riding whip, and
walked, no, strode along with it like a prince down
the wide central street between the barracks, the Boul-
evard des Misères, being religiously greeted (there is
no other word): he was the lord over life and death.
Some of this reverence naturally descended to me,
walking behind him, his adjutant. His Sancho Panza?
Well, hardly – at most a bit of a Leporello. But I did
it; I did not find it unpleasant. You thought it was
nice, come on, Jacob, admit it. Sure enough, it gave
me a pleasing tingle. Plainly I was already beginning
to be a man.

The Disposition Service: Cohn's masterly organization. A scant hundred men, popularly known as the
Jewish SS. This was a telling thrust, since we were
both Jews and SS, completely infected by our enemies,
whom we imitated in gait, in posture, in clothing,

even in our manner of speech: *"zackig"*, *"schneidig"*, — "real soldiers", "with plenty of zip". We chewed out, we shouldered aside, we rounded up. We, a few intellectuals, office clerks, workmen, travelling salesmen and pedlars, were to the others undoubtedly the most loathsome scum that God had ever created, cut-throats and gangsters; even now, this minute, I am sickened when I think back to us, to myself. The one thing I want to repeat for the tenth, for the hundredth time is that all this is true, that it was thus and not otherwise. Don't ask me any more about it, I just don't know. As I write, I realize more and more that at most I can still recognize myself. But as for knowing myself, that I don't, truly not.

Westerbork, *morne plaine*. Today as usual there is a storm, as there is practically the whole year; today as usual the pitiless sand is driving from the heath through every crevice in the barracks. At school I had picked up the notion that Holland, cosily surveyed and gradually built up until it was full, included no further inhospitable terrain; here they found the only one remaining, and here they planted a camp: "You need goggles here worse than you do food," Cohn had said, "look at the eyes of those infants, and imagine what fun it is here when summer comes with the billions of flies. And still they don't want to go to Auschwitz."

But it is all too true. I keep blowing the sand off this paper. Just one thing: it is quiet here, so far. No crying children, no disturbance, no chance, for instance, of the innumerable, completely senseless moves from barracks to barracks (*schnell, schnell!*);

28

nothing but the normal quantity of sand, dust, dirt, wet, and drafts. It is quiet here; so far, I said. Because half an hour ago the first addition turned up, a doctor's family, man, wife, and two children, including Betsy van Witsen from Class 2A. From 2A – here those numbers are a joke; we have a lot higher ones than that . . . There was no "race pollution" by *her* mother to judge by the look of her, but her father, a doctor on an emergency case, an accident around the corner, dashed out of the house with no star on his too-hastily donned jacket; the neighbour who reported it is already installed in their apartment, on which he had long had his eye. An ordinary punitive case, in other words. So even the knowledge of Goejanverwelle Lock could not save Betsy from Auschwitz, and there they sit at the other end of our barracks. Calm people, happy; how can it be possible? "Too bad," says her mother, "that we wound up in the punitive barracks, because I hear there's a good revue running in camp here. Have you seen it yet, Mr Henriques?"

I keep writing and writing. The words are willing to come now, so let's get on with it. I write: in this valley of death there is a cabaret, and there is even a café. A cabaret for which Schaufinger's buyers scoured the country to pick up the smartest costumes, the most modern lighting equipment; a cabaret with first-rate performers who rehearse all day; its first nights offer the most colourful show in all Europe, with rows of painted and primped female flesh, and Schaufinger as *le roi qui s'amuse* among them, along with Cohn, Schwarz, and the other VIPs. The opening is preferably, but not always, on a Tuesday evening, when a train has just gone, to cheer us up a little, evidently, a program of merriment and macabre humour on top of the sewer from which the Jews are discharged into the Acheron. You attend, or you stay away: which is the more normal, the less frantic? And those who shun the cabaret still sit in the café, the café, with terrace, with coffee (an ersatz substitute for laundry bleach), with lemonade; this is a perfectly matter-of-fact statement I'm writing, I'm not going wild, I'm reporting. Help me, Jacob, stand by me; I need your help indeed. In the café I arrested somebody one afternoon. Heavens, there the word is; let's count: just eight letters: arrested. How do you make an arrest? I had never seen it done, but done it had to be: orders from Cohn, orders from Schaufinger. Orders are orders: make the arrest. A Jew boy, a perfectly ordinary one, but with a trifle more bad luck, a trifle quicker bad luck than the other Jew boys here; they all go in the end. His premature bad luck lay in Schaufinger's foul temper that day; that sort of thing always costs human lives, even though he is, as Cohn keeps insisting, the most humane camp commandant of all, a little office worker swept to the surface by chance, who would ordinarily have been a little bookkeeper or cashier all his days. He is no monster, though I know very well that there is no occasion for that here: here he can live in a big house, with the whole camp working for him; no petty princeling ever had so many or such accomplished tailors, barbers, gardeners, chauffeurs, doctors, dentists, and so on; they celebrate his birthday here, and he graciously receives from Cohn's hands the Jewish birthday present. The best cooks prepare his meals, the finest mechanics devise toys for his children and those of his friends, and not long ago the leading calligrapher in Holland made him a gem of a family tree, of course an utterly Aryan one; all this was and is done by the Jews, his slaves. Naturally the prince maintains a sort of etiquette in his own way, and this was just the difficulty that noon. Anyway, his little dog, or rather that of his royal mistress, Frau Wirth (a prize bitch herself, by the way), the dog Bubi had been disrespectfully approached by one of his own kind inside the camp. Because sure enough – I can't help it if this story resembles Dostoevski's *House of the Dead* here and there – in this house of death there were still for a while people who possessed nothing in the world, but who starved themselves to pamper and spoil some animal, often as lean and sickly as themselves, dogs, cats, all the way to birds and turtles. A Jewish dog had forgotten himself with regard to Bubi, and there it was: final decree: all animals in the camp to be disposed of within one hour.

This was at quarter past one, and at quarter past two Schaufinger and Cohn went on their rounds of inspection as usual, I following behind Cohn. Schaufinger, as always, punctilious, erect, dashing – in passing I overheard one little Jewess say to another, "Isn't he good-looking today, though?" This he was, but also out of temper because la Wirth had wakened him from his midday nap. In the first barracks it happened: a Jew boy was there, washing, but when he saw the three of us, he flew into a panic, naturally not being a Doctor of History, and shyly planted a star on his completely bare breast with a piece of plaster, on the left side according to regulations. Schaufinger saw it, and went on; somewhere in another barracks he discovered a kitten ostensibly without an owner, calmly and decisively put his military boot on it, and had six people from that building put on the transport list. I repeat, for a camp commandant he is not a monster, he is sometimes downright *gemütlich*, and then he may even speak a few words of Yiddish, but this once he was somewhat put out, and so that afternoon, when he had evidently given the matter careful thought, I was ordered to arrest Isaiah Melkman, born May 11, 1923, furrier by trade, and bring him to punitive barracks on the charge of insulting a symbol. This was a transgression of which Isaiah Melkman, furrier by trade, will hardly have understood anything, even aboard the train, and no more will his girl, who voluntarily accompanied him. But to Jacques Suasso Henriques, teacher by profession, it is not altogether clear either; only Jacob whispers: Isaiah, Isaiah. What do you mean, Jacob?

In writing I have already wasted too much time on this unimportant episode; if I keep on this way, I shall need weeks, and I have only a few days more.

So let us not repeat the story of Father: it happened that we had to help clear out a couple of rest homes in Amsterdam; I've already written something about that – don't do it again, says Jacob, but don't forget it. Mother: thanks to my position with Cohn she could have stayed a long time in Westerbork, but when she heard about Father she took leave of her wits: she swore up and down that she had been a foundling, that I, her son, was born of adultery, that her husband, Father, that is, was not my own father, that she herself was of exalted descent, and so on. She could probably have accomplished nothing with a single argument, but this hodgepodge was hopeless, particularly when she dared to accost Schaufinger in person, who for Jews, excepting Cohn, was as much taboo as the Mikado of Japan. This irrevocably meant the train, and the only thing I could still do for her was to get her a good seat between the water cask and the cask for excrement; I can still hear the sarcastic "Heils" that greeted her in the car.

A good seat was in fact sometimes the most one could do. Thus for Uncle Felix, already mentioned, with Aunt Hannah and her backward children. Thus for our doctor, the "angel" as Father always called him, our doctor, counsellor, and friend even before my birth. He had been betrayed by his former chauffeur because, hurrying homeward from a confinement, he had reached his front door just five minutes after eight. He came with a whole separate shipment from a camp for the training of our Dutch SS, and there, as was not unusual, they had set dogs on them; at any rate scraps of flesh were still hanging loose, with a dab of mercury ointment here and there on the wounds. I had to support him like a child, and as I write I can see his good, kind eyes fixed upon me as he took mute farewell, to crouch down, aching in every limb, beside the excrement bucket; God cannot have seen this more plainly than I. And then? One Tuesday morning the train was ready when suddenly Meiersohn, our chief physician, beckoned to Cohn: he wanted to defer a young woman on account of pregnancy, which at that time still entitled a woman to a delay of six weeks from the confinement (at that time; afterward I often put women next to the bucket shortly before they gave birth). Cohn, standing rigidly at attention (to Schaufinger): "I beg to report, Herr Obersturmbannführer, young woman off the list." Schaufinger: "Too bad. Then that makes . . ." Cohn: "That makes nine hundred and sixty-nine, Herr Obersturmbannführer!" Schaufinger: "One too few. Oh, well. Next time . . ." Cohn: "Excuse me, Herr Obersturmbannführer. You ordered nine hundred and seventy, you're going to get your nine hundred and seventy." And without awaiting an answer from Schaufinger (who did smile contentedly) he wrote a name on a sheet of paper from a pad, and rasped: "Suasso! Hut seventy-two. Remember, be quick about it!"

When I unfolded my slip of paper in the barracks, I was far from suspecting that Sadie de Vries, born January 27, 1925, was in fact Ninon. Those wide eyes, that ashy-pale little face – only later did I realize how unexpectedly it had happened. Old Nathan de Vries, guaranteed the wiliest Jewish diamond dealer in either hemisphere, had blundered into the silliest trap: for ten thousand guilders per person an escape to Switzerland, which reached its natural end by betrayal to the Gestapo no further than Maastricht. Anything that cost that much could not be worth anything – surely any half-wit knew that! Once caught, he had indeed saved what could be saved, for instance spending a few more tens of thousands to get the dreaded P (for Punitive Barracks) removed from their identification papers; for as much again – I can't help it if all this grows tiresome – he had even acquired a rubber stamp that was supposed to exempt the family from deportation; thus he was on a list, and on a good one. And now came this. I should add that I had not yet noticed them in this village with its shifting population; I was just as startled as they. As they, I say, because naturally her father and mother joined us forthwith, he nervously fumbling with a paper, purple with stamp ink, and with signatures in the familiar angular script. I saw only one recourse: Cohn. Thither we went, Ninon and I in the lead. She was trembling so that I gave her my arm, which she clutched against her breast; her teeth were chattering. And now I must put something down here; I must put it into words, I must say something absolutely indispensable, or else I can't go on; I shall have to tear this up again. God, dear God, I *must* write this: never had I been so inexpressibly in love with her as during that short passage along the barracks, through the mud – and she had only a pair of little pumps on, and not even a coat, and dear God, dear God, she shivered like a little bird. *Pavane pour une infante défunte* – let that serve to express it. "Are they really going to send me away, Mr Henriques?" "Put a bold face on it, Ninon, that's your one chance." Into the dark inferno: *taciti, soli, senza compagnia* – Dante,

35

yours was a bleak sort of hell. This is how it all happened; God help me, I can do no other, this is the truth that I could not write down before. There we stood before Cohn, two paces further away Schaufinger, playing with the dog Bubi, which was never absent at the train, and was darting about him with short barks. Identification papers! – alas, they covered only the parents and the children under eighteen: born January 27, 1925. Cohn decided: into the car at once, quick, quick! And: "Come on, Suasso, be a proper gallant, lend the young lady a hand!"

Was I a man? The little girl, for such she suddenly was again, the little girl flung herself into the mud, embracing my knees. "Come on, Suasso! Get on with it! Let's go!" I lifted her up with difficulty and carried her in my arms, against my pounding heart, to the only car that was still standing open. *Ce goût de terre et de mort, ce poids sur le coeur, c'est tout ce qui reste pour moi de la grande aventure, et de vous, Yvonne de Galais, jeune femme tant cherchée – tant aimée* . . . Our being is nothing, completely nothing, nothing, nothing. Behind us I heard her father yell, not to Cohn, but to Schaufinger: "But I'm not going to let my daughter go to perdition alone, what are you thinking of?"

And Schaufinger, accommodating as always: "But you're welcome to get aboard, sir. Madame will go too, of course. *Bon voyage!*"

And at a sign two Disposition Service men thrust the old couple into the same car, the door slid shut with a bang, there was the shrill whistle of every Tuesday, and the epilogue of Schaufinger: "Well, Mr Cohn, you've actually got nine hundred seventy-two. Come on, Bubi!" This last to the dog.

I was not a man yet, I said. But after all, it was a long road: two evenings before, I had been on duty during the clearing out of the Oppenheimer Foundation, the Jewish Institution for the Insane at Deventer. A few must have escaped, both orderlies and inmates, and I hope some day someone can tell the story, even an illiterate or a lunatic, because I cannot. Adelphi from Amsterdam was in charge himself, and had applied to Schaufinger for a couple of dozen of us to help. And so, through the pitch-black night, we carried stark-naked, yelling lunatics, their arms tied, to the cars; when I paused an instant to vomit, Adelphi himself fetched me a kick: "Faster, Jew!" And we ran faster, and flung the naked woman, still violently kicking and screeching, on a number of human bodies already hurled to the floor of the car, some smeared with blood, others with excrement. My crew, because I was in charge – naturally someone had to be in charge as usual – my crew sighed, wept, and cursed as they went, but still kept stacking as if they were loading parcels. Incidentally, there were among these patients not a few normal individuals – normal, but still crazy enough to suppose in their innocence that a nation of poets and thinkers could emulate the primitive peoples to whom the insane are taboo and an object of care and affection. In Deventer nothing could happen to you, they had promised, and, so thinking, a girl from my Class 5B had also found refuge here, and accordingly, just like the others, was heaved into the car, screaming horribly. Yes, Mona, heaved in; I can't remember your last name, and that is probably erased for all time: no tombstone for you, Mona. You were the little mother of 5B, you sat on the first bench on the window side; you were so well-mannered and good-hearted. Here I'm talking a little to you, Mona, among the naked lunatics in a sealed cattle car with the ventilation closed, rolling into the abyss. How strange, Mona, my little Jewish sister, how strange that I was actually able to write down the part about Ninon, after all, little by little, but that now I sit crying out loud, here at this table, out loud, and that I have got to stop because my eyes are blind with hot tears.

THE PLACE IS FILLING UP, and I can see I must go on with the job. Quite a number of children today, dull and weary, petulant and crying, all punitive cases, even an infant in arms, all for labour service in Germany; what their offences were I do not know, and anyway it is irrelevant. I cannot say that my former colleagues, the chosen turnkeys of this unique prison, are pleasant to them; as I have already remarked, we were scum, offscourings. We, I say, because I was part of it, although now I am struck by how little *esprit de corps* there was among us. Oh, well, ultimately we had only one bond – with Cohn. Not even common barracks. Cohn himself explained this last to me in one of our first conversations.

"Look, Suasso," he began, "let's count the Germans here. A dozen, no more. And they, with the help of a few undependable men from the constabulary, are supposed to guard a whole Jewish village. You can see that there's a problem there, right?"

"Hardly, sir. A thousand Jews would run away from a single SS man."

Cohn smiled. "Georg has already written to me about your . . . well, about your ambivalence. But you're forgetting a couple of things, Suasso. Really you are. For instance you're forgetting that the first groups in Amsterdam to fight the Dutch Nazis were full of Jews. And you're forgetting that there's such a thing as a Jewish Underground."

Now it was my turn to smile.

"You're wrong, Suasso," he went on, "quite wrong. Funny how the Dutch anti-Semites overestimate the Jewish resistance just as much as the Germans under-estimate it. Don't make any mistake."

"Here in camp they're mostly pretty subdued, Mr Cohn."

"What do you expect, Suasso? Open rebellion? Well, all right, then I suppose the dozen Germans actually would bite the dust, and Cohn, Schwarz, and possibly Suasso with them for company. But then? What next? No, Suasso. There's quite a different resist-ance at work here. Did you know that people regularly escape from here?"

I looked incredulous. "From here?"

"From here. In spite of sentries, machine-guns, barbed wire, supervision, roll calls, card systems, and registration. I sometimes ask myself whether the very perfection of the system isn't what makes the leaks possible. But leaks there are, and I can't put up with them. Naturally Schaufinger knows about it; otherwise Schwarz or somebody would have whispered it to him in order to take my seat. But Schaufinger also knows that Schwarz isn't a jot better. Schwarz is a petty crook, Rosenfeld a schemer, Goldstein a roughneck, and

Sacher is too well-mannered – he's the most impossible of us all."

"But what are you afraid of then, sir?"

"Of Schaufinger, naturally. Some fine day he may get his bellyful after all. Or The Hague will say, put Cohn aboard the train and keep looking until you discover the Jew who can solve the escapes. As long as that danger threatens, I've got to be the Jew. The Disposition Service has got to help me – each one of you in a different building."

"As an observer."

"As a spy, Suasso, as a common, ordinary spy. No pretty words here: as a spy. Nothing you ever dreamed of in your teaching days, hey? You go into the buildings according to the roster, mix with the women and children. You listen, you report. You'll be playing cops and robbers, but think of the stake in the game. Success means promotion. Lack of success may mean Auschwitz along with Cohn. Not round trip, one way. Auschwitz Spa. You'll do better to stay here in the moors, take it from me."

ND THAT WAS HOW my wanderings
through the barracks began. A moment ago I mentioned Dante, but the dry stick I am lacks faith in his
hell. In this one I do believe. Completely. Those are
facts to me, and the only thing I am now gradually
beginning to understand is that I should really be able
to include the facts within the scheme of a satanic myth
if I hope to communicate their actuality and reality to
others, my reader or readers.

This hell exists today alone. There is no past and no
future; everyone knows that in his heart. The past is
dead; the future is death. Between the two lies the
narrow watershed, life. And that life consists of looking
for a shoelace, of quarrelling over a seat by the stove,
of fleeting encounters with a woman on the barter
system, of intolerable loneliness in intolerable crowds.
Each week it rises anew to the fiercest, the unspeakably
grisly horror of the one night, the night before the
departure: the apocalyptic plunge, forever new, of hundreds of human beings into destruction and death.

How STRANGE! A good two weeks ago, eighteen days to be exact, I started on my first account, possibly ten days later on my second, both failures. Well, after a lot of jolting and bumping at the start – rereading it, I can laugh at this – it is moving along; each word snaps into place with a click, forgotten things rise to the surface, connections become visible. For instance the day now pops into my mind when I myself became aware of the urge to write that possesses so many of those who live here, and it is hardly by chance, I now realize, that this was also the day of the silly incident between Cohn and Red Hein, the one untrustworthy constable. Cohn, in jacket and boots, was carrying out an inspection when Hein roared at him: "Stop! Come over here! Yes, you! Don't you know how to salute?" Cohn, who actually had not noticed him, promptly recognized the danger, clicked his heels, and stood straight as a ramrod, stiff, cap in hand. "Answer me, kike!" "My apologies, Captain, I was thinking about something else, I . . ." "I don't need your apologies, kike! If it happens again I'll report it! And now, dismiss!" I could feel the eyes of all the camp inmates upon us as Cohn, executing a smart

43

about-turn, marched off; I tasted their enjoyment, their malicious pleasure, their derision. The pseudo hierarchy came tumbling down at the first shove from the pettiest Philistine. It was glorious to them, naturally, but that it was glorious was now precisely the abhorrent part (I can feel it more now than then).

Strange: this trifling occurrence – it wasn't so trifling, Jacob insists – led to my closer acquaintance with the "Rabbi". That was what I called him, following a conversation overheard in barracks (I eavesdropped much and attentively), but we had never exchanged a word; now I still call him so, though I know from his own lips that he was not a rabbi at all, not even a *moré*. How this last came about he once explained, in one of his innumerable anecdotes, after we had grown intimate.

"You've never had half an hour's Jewish teaching in all your life, Henriques. Well, you know how I feel about that. Anyway, religious instruction is my speciality; when you stop to think about it, we are really colleagues in a way – I hope you won't mind my saying so. Well, anyhow, that wasn't what I started to talk about. One day the Raaf came into one of my classes – I suppose you know who the Raaf is? No? All right, it's the Chief Rabbi. A fine man, Henriques, not a word against the Raaf, a fine person, but strict, you have no idea. Now I just happened to have a gem of a subject for the children. Too bad you've never read a word of the Bible in your life, because you find that story right near the beginning. Look it up some time when you're off duty, in *Genesis* XIX: Abraham bargaining with the Judge of the whole world, asking if he will spare the city of Sodom if there are fifty righteous men in it, and then, having gained that, if there are forty-five, and so on down to ten. Well, and I was so caught up in the spirit of my lesson that I went down to five . . ."

"You probably thought five were enough, yourself."

"Right you are, Henriques, blessings on you. Even one seems to me plenty. After all, you can see any day on this camp how easy it is for anyone to be unrighteous in Sodom and Gomorrah, can't you? Well, to get back to my story, I overshot my target, so to speak, or rather the finish line, and I went on to five. In came the Raaf. After the lesson he called me in, and gave it to me straight: 'Mr Hirsch! You're teaching the children completely wrong. If Abraham stopped at ten righteous men, you have no business to go on to five! The cheek of it! I was planning to give you the title of *moré*, but that's out of the question for the time being. And I was thinking of raising your salary by two hundred and fifty guilders. You won't get that either.'"

"Quite a punishment!"

"Well, that was how it went in the Jewish Congregation; naturally you have no idea of that. Let me tell you, though, that the title of *moré* didn't bother me, but for each of those Sodomites to cost me fifty guilders I did think was a shame."

We both laughed. In fact I laughed a great deal with the "Rabbi"; in that camp I never really laughed except with him, for amusement or sociability. Because wherever he was, it was sociable — a rarity in any camp.

And this even though he was in Hut 52, the worst of them all, with a vile mood prevailing, more or less rock bottom. Any barracks crammed with people is a mass of greed, selfishness, lust for power, and meddlesomeness, and all these cravings are a sign of sickness. In any barracks decent, well-brought-up people can become tyrants, liars, ruffians, thieves in no time, but Hut 52 was really the end. The amount of rumours, nonsense, slander, and spite dished up in a single Sunday afternoon there would have filled a good-sized scandal sheet. One ought to take it down in shorthand, as the German wit Tucholsky said. But here too was the amazing phenomenon: one person accomplishing the impossible, and not only remaining sound within himself, but radiating spiritual health around him. I had been posted in Hut 52 as a spy a couple days before his arrival, having failed to find anything in previous barracks. Even for Hut 52 Cohn offered me little hope, because he realized perfectly well that the soil for subversive activity was lacking: "The more bellyaching, the less resistance," he said, and it's obvious enough. The arrival of Jeremiah Hirsch did not, of course, immediately alter the general temper. And yet, in some way that I could never trace and still cannot understand, his presence "took effect" from the start; he was not a rabbi or a *moré*, and still something played a part that is certainly not found in Jews alone: in his presence you were somewhat constrained, embarrassed, even though in his absence you could go on hacking away at his office and those who held it, as familiarly or hatefully as you pleased. And as you got more and

46

more used to him, you were more and more embarrassed. And behaved yourself better. Strange. For me the whole thing was a peculiar experience: this was the first Jewish clergyman I had ever met; the subject was never mentioned at home, and Mother's Remonstrant parson had not been the man to interest me much in his Jewish colleagues. As I said, I had heard him called a *rebbe*, and the word, with its touch of derision, had stuck in my mind; it had a different sort of sound from the formal term. But that cannot have been his only introduction to me. In every way, I am only now coming to realize, he was the very opposite of Cohn, fine-drawn and small-boned, with a high forehead and what in a different period used to be called a noble countenance; he limped somewhat, a result of infantile paralysis, and I can no more imagine him in a uniform than Cohn out of one. Particularly his eyes, large and dark, were splendid; his voice was controlled and melodious. And naturally he did not wear Cohn's dashing barracks cap, but an inconspicuous little skull-cap. I repeat: our first conversation came immediately after Cohn's humiliation by Red Hein. He was standing at the entrance to the barracks, among some fellow sufferers whose malicious delight fairly dripped·from their chops until it made my hands itch. I had a great longing to sweep them into the punitive barracks where I am sitting now.

He looked straight at me, and said, pointing to Cohn: "Poor man! I wouldn't like to change places with him."

"I rather think not," I said venomously. "Do you

imagine nothing like that could ever happen to you? As if you amounted to anything compared with a brute like Red Hein! Let me tell you that Mr Cohn is still better off than you by a good deal." There, that went home.

He remained quite placid, though. "I realize that perfectly, Mr Henriques – that's your name, isn't it? My name is Hirsch. You don't need to tell me who and what Mr Cohn is, at least inside this camp. I know, possibly I know better than you. And that's why I say again, I wouldn't care to trade with him. He's to be pitied, because he can't do anything back, nothing at all."

"And what can you do back, pray tell?"

"Do you really want to know?"

"Very much." Yes, Jacob, I said very much, because, you know, after all I was a spy, an ordinary informer, and I had to get about my job. You'll tell me that it wasn't quite so, but a little different by this time. Possibly; I only hope so.

"Good, Mr Henriques. You don't know any Hebrew, I presume. No? Not a word, you say? Too bad, too bad, but I supposed as much. We'll manage, though, even so. Just come with me; beside the plank bed there is my library, Westerbork Branch. Just a second." He turned pages, speaking aside to a couple of inquisitive fellow inmates: "Come on and join us; we have no secrets from you people. Too bad there aren't ten of you." Ten was the minimum number of men for a religious service. "Wait, here it is," he went on. "You definitely want to know, do you, Mr

Henriques? Yes? All right, but in that case I have one request to make of you: please read out loud what it says here. See, this is from the *Book of Joshua*. Never looked at it before, I imagine. No. Just you read out loud, word by word, a little slow, so the others can hear too."

And I read: "For the Lord thy God is with thee whithersoever thou goest." I saw his lips moving; very softly he was muttering something along with me that I did not understand.

"Thank you, Mr Henriques. That's it. You asked me what I could do back. I didn't answer your question exactly, because that is what *we* can do back. And I don't suppose you'll be satisfied with it, but I think you'll come back to it some time. If you choose, naturally. Not now, because I work in the sorting shop, and this is my time. My wife is there too; she's quartered with our twins in Hut 16, even closer to the latrines and with even more modern conveniences. I'm sure you'll excuse me, Mr Henriques. Oh, by the way, if you want to read any more, it's next to the bunk. You'll always find it there. That's probably the only thing nobody in this whole camp will ever swipe."

How often did we talk to one another after that? And what about? All at once I feel the lack of a Boswellian memory: all the conversations in this account are of necessity reconstructions, in which of course I try to reproduce accurately, yet even if involuntarily I am bound the bungle it. It's too bad that we didn't make a recording (the very idea, in a place like this!), because then I would not only have preserved the timbre of his voice, but could also now trace out why it was that in almost every conversation we moved in the same direction, without my perceiving the slightest touch of missionary zeal in him, and this in a man who would not boast the sporting open-mindedness that characterized Mother's parson. Not infrequently the starting point was a joke, a challenging remark on his part, but all at once five minutes later we would be in the midst of a conversation, a real, a "deep" conversation. How he managed it is still a mystery to me, but almost always we reached the conclusion of the first time; to the others it was probably a silly performance – I in my SS uniform reading out loud, and the Rabbi facing me, mumbling along with me, just as before, in his incomprehensible tongue; I presume that they regarded us, or at least me, as a silly idiot, as the *"meshuggene* Portuguese" that I was by origin, and more than once there was whispering and suppressed laughter. But I also remember how perfectly still it was around us the one time when at his request I began reading out the Twenty-third Psalm, for at the words, "though I walk through the valley of the shadow of death," I could not go on, so that he took the book from my hand and continued in a low but clear voice, now speaking Dutch.

I AM STILL SITTING at this table, but it grows more and more impossible to write. No, my association with the "Rabbi" most certainly did not turn me into a saint; I am having difficulty in refraining from bursting out into the hub-bub and yelling at my fellow inmates, "If you're going to perdition in a couple of days anyway, you might at least start now by shutting up for a while." This applies particularly to some new cases (we are practically crammed full here), the former inmates of a rest home for old ladies who are guilty of heaven knows what, and have wound up in this building; there are only a dozen of them, but together they more or less amount to the Thousand-year Reich, except for the quiet we can expect there. They gabble all day about the silver plate they used to have, the stair carpet they used to have, their maids ditto, the you-name-it ditto. They simply have no notion, no concept, no faint suspicion. I can't even feel that the "Rabbi" has made me into a philo-Semite – possibly a trifle less of an anti-Semite, and certainly into rather more of a Jew, though goodness knows what that means. We talked about that, too, he and I; we plunged right into the middle of it by way of the customary joke. It was one cabaret evening after an abominable train-load, made up entirely of old people, full of invalids and with a large number of the blind, for which the clearing out of the Jewish Institute for the Blind at Amsterdam had supplied the material. We as Disposition Service had our hands full, particularly because Cohn, goaded by Schaufinger, kept at us even more viciously than usual; naturally he wanted to get rid of these helpless people as quickly as possible himself, and sulkily rasped order after order at us. It was a relief when they were all well and truly (well and truly, Jacob whispers) settled in the car, shoved in by several of us; I can still see the tears in the dead eyes of a very old little woman when Cohn gave her a cut across the hands with his riding whip, for what reason I do not know. I was completely out of sorts and longing for distraction, and was on my way to the cabaret when I bumped into the Rabbi outside the building, and invited him somewhat archly to accompany me.

As was his habit, he did not reply immediately. "Come along? All right. But on one condition: that they're putting on an opera."

"Listen to me, Hirsch. I assure you Schaufinger will see to that, too, before he's done. Possibly *Fidelio* — what would you think of that? It takes place in a prison, too."

"Well, Henriques, I'm not quite sure. I'll need to take a closer look. Beethoven was no Jew, but still he could have been an honorary Jew for the final chorus of the Ninth. *Alle Menschen werden Brüder*, all men shall be brothers. Not Schaufinger's style. He might just as

well begin straight off with Offenbach or Meyerbeer."
(Jews were only permitted to perform the music of Jewish composers in public).

"Meyerbeer? No thanks!"

"Yes, naturally you're aping Richard Wagner, another Jew-lover for you. No, my boy, that Meyerbeer wasn't so *meshugge* as you think. Anyway, even if he didn't write the most beautiful opera there ever was, still it was the most likeable. To me, anyway. And, if you stop to think, to you, too."

"Stop your fooling. What one do you mean?"

"*The Huguenots*. You weren't expecting that, were you? But do you know why? I learned that from my late lamented father: he always said, give me *The Huguenots* every time. A splendid opera, splendid. The Protestants and the Catholics kill each other off, and a Jew wrote the music to it. What more could you ask?"

I laughed. "Are you so disgusted with the Protestants and the Catholics?" I asked.

"Me? With the *goyim?* No, of course not, what put that into your head? That was just a joke. Disgusted? Not at all, really, possibly rather less than you, my boy."

"How strange you should say that."

"Strange? Am I right or am I wrong?"

"Yes, at least partly. Partly. I have a feeling that at least recently I've been growing toward this country, take note, toward the *country*. I belong here and nowhere else. But the people? No, I wouldn't say that. In fact I think I'm becoming estranged from the people. The *people*, that is. Do you feel it too?"

54

"I know just what you mean. And I say no. No, and no again."

"Then it's very strange indeed. You as a Jew, as an orthodox Jew . . ."

"Aren't you a Jew?"

"Of course! Don't you see me wearing a star? Am I not in Westerbork?" Naturally I meant it ironically, but either this escaped him or he pretended it did; at any rate he hastily interrupted, "Exactly, my boy, exactly: that's why you're a Jew. Not only for that reason, of course, but the other reasons will probably come later, when you've got a bit further along, and have graduated from Jewish Dutchman to Dutch Jew. That's still quite a stretch, I can feel that plainly; so let's confine ourselves to today. Today you and I as Jews, joined by a common fate, are behind the barbed wire. You have no idea how much barbed wire there is in our Jewish history – it's a regular barbed idyll. But it's a tight bond, all right. When you get caught in it. And that you do, sooner or later."

"But you were going to show me . . ."

"Oh, yes, that's right; we hadn't finished with your question. One thing more: I'm not estranged from the Jews, of course not, but neither am I from the others. I mean, from my fellow men."

"Not even from the Germans?"

He bowed his head. I waited in suspense. For another moment he hesitated, but at last he said softly, "Not even from the Germans." And then, little by little a bit louder: "Oh, Henriques, you have no idea how difficult it is, and I only hope I can hold on to

55

that. After all, I'm only human, too. You know my Leah is in 16 with Ben and Judith. That's the worst one there is. I'll just have to try. Lend me a hand; it needn't be all the time, but now and then, if only for a moment. Keep putting your trust in your fellow men. And particularly in the ordinary folk."

"A fine lot they are here, these ordinary folk. When you look around you . . ."

"Yes, yes. Do you think I'm deaf, dumb, and blind? I'm not idealizing anybody or anything. I lived for years among the poorest of the poor – *mon curé chez les pauvres*. But even here, which is worse than Sodom and Gomorrah combined, even here you find a few of the righteous. Not so very many, but anyway more than you and your kind . . ."

"My kind?"

"Yes. Mr Henriques, you and your kind. Look angry if you like; I know precisely what I'm saying. People of your kind (are you listening carefully?) always look down on ordinary folk. It's your kind that first despatches the ordinary folk to Poland; first the people who wear flat caps, and then the people who wear hats. If you weren't half a fascist yourself, you could have proved it out of Marx; I never studied economics, so I just get along with another book that you haven't read either. But that tells you exactly, not only how tempting a thing of that kind can be, but how abominable it is. Well, you're gradually discovering where you can find it: next to my bunk. Then you can read with your own eyes how good it is to trust in the common people, and you'll learn that the opposite, that pride of yours, gets you nowhere."

That evening I did not go to the cabaret, because I stayed behind and read. Still, I know from camp gossip what happened. The revue, newly rehearsed, with new and scandalously costly settings, was the biggest success of a highly successful season, already rich in first-rate performances. Probably the chief hit was the latest popular song, sung in unison by the entire audience, "Kurt, Kurt, He loves us like his children." Schaufinger, Kurt Schaufinger, highly flattered, summoned the soubrette, Lizzy Heine, and praised her with the greatest superlative he could use: "What a shame, Fräulein, that you are Jewish!" Lizzy was generally envied. Less than two weeks later she was aboard the train.

THE TRAIN. I cannot escape the word any longer; it was bound to come, and now it is here; I have a feeling it will stay till the end of the story.

The train. Aldous Huxley somewhere called the masculine soul in its immature stage *naturaliter ferrovialis*, and, remembering my own youth, I can say it is true. Children are by nature train-minded, they have a fondness for trains. More than that, for years I felt strangely moved when one of these mighty machines rolled into the station; I thought it was superb. I can still see myself, one vacation at Zandvoort, preferring to spend my time watching the trains at the station rather than on the beach. That was the boy, the unlikely little individual, that I must have been. But now I have indeed matured according to the Cohn plan, for I no longer feel in the least *ferrovialis*, and I shall never be able to feel so again; to me, after all, this camp has turned the train into a symbol of suffering and unhappiness, of death, no, of evil itself. And evil I have learned to hate. From the "Rabbi", Jacob whispers. It may be; certainly he had something to do with it.

The train, the train. It comes and it goes, but even more unendurable than the arrivals, than the departures, is the regularity with which these take place. Let it storm, snow, freeze to sheet ice; the train goes. No air-raid alarm stops it; the train goes. Our Allies smash whole railway junctions, destroy bridges and hangars, repair shops and materiel, but the train goes. There was a strike in Amsterdam over the removal of a few hundred Jews, but here it is constantly carrying away thousands, and everyone does his duty, and not a soul objects; not a sleeper is out of place, not a bolt loosened.

The train is the Devil. As it looms up out of the darkness with its dully glaring headlights, as it shrieks its triumph over us with a shrill whistle, as it moves slowly banging and rumbling along the platform, and finally comes to a stop with a hot hissing and a quivering reverberation, it is like a prehistoric monster of enormous strength, the dragon from an evil fairy tale. Suddenly it is in the midst of the camp, conjured up as by a magic spell out of Hades. In one respect Georg was certainly right: compared to this train the guillotine is a toy, a piece of Louis XVI bric-à-brac.

And then remember that it appears only in the fourth and fifth acts — acts of the tragedy that plays here once a week (just once it was twice a week), a drama that is always the same and yet different each time. But the moment the demon comes thundering up out of the abyss, everyone feels its silent presence, as inescapable as the resounding trumpets of the Last Judgment.

The drama starts Sunday noon. In Act I, there occurs the phenomenon once tellingly described by Cohn as follows: the rumour-projector makes a 180-degree turn. All week it is directed at the world outside, chiefly at the war news. It knows what cities have been taken, what Churchill's plans are, how deeply Mussolini is mired. Stopping to think about it now, I conclude that it is not even untruthful; what it proclaims is the truth, but the future truth; it states, where it ought to prophesy. The cities it has falling will in fact be captured, but much later and, for most if not all of us, too late. But it is just the same here as at school: people want to believe briefly, to enjoy the fleeting daydream, to lull themselves in illusion. Sunday noon, then, it turns around, pointing inward, at us, at the coming days and hours, and then it does in fact become troublesomely inaccurate. "The train isn't coming." It always comes. "Schaufinger's gone." Schaufinger is here as usual, and the one time when he was on leave Frau Wirth (with Bubi as usual) did the job better, and with a heavier hand, than he. "They are going to exchange us." Jews are evidently too precious or too worthless to be exchanged for anything whatsoever. "The government in London has got to . . . Sweden may . . . Stalin intends . . . Roosevelt can . . . Churchill is expected to . . ." From all these certainties at least one logical line leads to the next certainty: this week there will be no train. The train does come, naturally, always. The clock may stop, but the train comes.

Monday noon, every week, meeting at Schaufinger's. Order of the day: a neat shave, boots polished, every button in place, as if for a ceremony. And such indeed it properly is; I once toyed with the blasphemous thought that the affair ought to start with prayer. The round table is ready for the session – of the Council of Blood, says Jacob. The camp commandant is the only one without a star – just like Napoleon without a single decoration among his gold-laden field marshals, the only man with authority. Here the field marshals are the six or seven Service supervisors, with Cohn as chief of staff and me as his adjutant behind him. Everything top secret: the penalty for a whisper is the next train. But the camp has an incalculably immense interest in knowing what threatens – how many must go to the block, and who. How many, that is the number. The number is like 666 in the *Book of Revelation*; the number appears, the number rules, the number *is*. The number of the beast is in *Revelation* (three months ago I would have known nothing about it); in truth, the number of the Beast. We know only too well whence it comes, and realize that no more can be done about it than about the barometer reading. A number in arithmetic may be composed of factors, but this camp number is made up of human beings, one by one, added together. All kinds of people, quite different, men and women, old and young, but all now united and set apart by a common trembling. Each individual member, I cannot repeat often enough, is a person, a human being. In terror, in mortal terror – and rightly so.

For we start counting. Cohn has his card ready, and screws the top off his fountain pen. First come those not on the embargo list. There are such, the pariahs in this strictly caste-structured community. Not on the embargo list: better to be a leper. The punitive barracks, our leprosarium, is of course included; these people are not only not on an embargo list, they are outcasts like myself now. With luck, this alone will furnish us our number for the week. But we are not always lucky. And labour service cannot wait, so that we have to scrape up the number from every nook and cranny of the camp. Then it is the ailing who set the pace. The more people in the punitive barracks, the fewer of the sick, that is obvious; if, for instance, a number of large families have been caught one week, the hospital inmates look cheerful; if not, they look glum. Evidently the sick must be particularly suited to labour service, because the sicker they are, the more defenceless, the sooner they get put on the list. But heaven help us if we still don't make up the number; then the fur starts to fly. Because then the lists go up in smoke, rubber-stamps prove invalid, identification documents are scrap paper: suddenly all the thousands of little dikes burst by which people, sometimes at an expenditure of thousands of guilders, had built up a little dream of safety.

Yes, the number sometimes gives the meeting a good deal of trouble. But we always get it together, and in the end it is usually not so bad, because naturally we ourselves remain here; we are, so to speak, on the list of ourselves. After this job we have to draw up a loading list, so and so many cattle-trucks, so and so many people; each truck with a leader, and these leaders jointly with a leader of their own; according to the Germans nothing can be done without a hierarchy, and gradually the Jews have come to think it the most natural thing in the world. There is also a transport physician, because a journey of several days and nights in an ill-ventilated cattle-truck might not agree with somebody: ". . . *und wir sind keine Unmenschen* – and we are not inhuman." Lucky that the Jews have practised medicine since time immemorial: doctors enough; I have already told how our family doctor went; he too was a transport physician. Then the meeting is finished, and we go, defying the classical unity of place, to the registry building. There they draw up the master list, the one with the number, down to the smallest details: the finished work. All the shipment-free names are removed from the file; shipment-free means free *for*, not *from* shipment: *vive la petite différence!* Or, if I must use a French quotation, *"A nous la liberté?"* Because although we know almost nothing about Auschwitz, at any rate word has reached here that a sign over the entrance gate says ARBEIT MACHT FREI – Work Makes You Free – and some of us think this a good sign.

The camp waits. Nobody knows anything, but still the number leaks out, heaven knows how. Another thing: nobody knows anything, but they suspect. Even the very safest has moments when he turns pale, when he feels the ground quaking for an instant under his feet, when he imagines himself threatened and feels the need of a dose of "Vitamin C" (for Connections). Because salvation must often come through Connections, yes, whenever a rubber stamp won't do the trick or a list comes apart. Cohn in particular is then very much in demand, but even his humble adjutant has repeatedly had offers in cash or barter that's made his ears ring, with a record figure, in money, of forty thousand guilders – simply for an audience with the mighty man. There are probably a couple of ladies who will look the other way if they ever meet me again in South Amsterdam – small chance of that.

Naturally hundreds of life-and-death cases are in progress, and the borderline cases in particular fight for their lives. They are scratched off the transport list, and then all of a sudden they are on it again, and this perhaps two, three, or even four times on one Monday, and the same person sometimes weeks in succession, until he finally sticks on some list and has to go, not seldom relieved, not seldom at his tether's end. Some day the cat catches the mouse; that is Camp Law Number Such-and-Such – I forget the number. In this same registry building the master list then has to be subdivided into separate rosters for the various buildings, in the midst of a witches' caldron where the screeching, haggling, and praying grows ever fiercer – a market in human lives. This goes on until late in the evening; usually we are not finished until about

64

midnight, and then the actual night of the transport can begin.

Oh night of nights! In vain I try to imagine how I lived through it over and over again, but I can't do it; if I could, I might fall down dead. I can only say that since then there has been nothing left of me; if I am still alive now, it is through something I do not know, that I cannot give a name to. The night of retribution, the night of judgment. I myself have repeatedly had to read out the list in my own building, and I well remember: my first names echoed in a silence – the Unthinkable before the Creation cannot have been stiller. It was as though the deaf listened to me, the blind looked at me, all rigid in supreme immobility. The list was alphabetical, but nobody quite depended on it; only when I was finished did bedlam break loose. I have seen people dancing, wild with joy, as though whirled by an elemental force, kissing and laying hands upon one another in the most obscene fashion; others I have seen running as if they had taken leave of their senses, falling down and getting up again, over and over, bumping into the benches, the tables, the walls, and finally lying there, kicking and hitting about them; I have seen a woman bite the jugular vein of her sister, whose name was not called, and who had thus escaped; and a man who put out his eyes right in front of me because another, three steps from me, was sitting sobbing with joy. I have seen it, seen it myself, many nights of perdition. I HAVE SEEN IT.

Act V takes place toward morning. The condemned

have packed, helped and generously supplied with everything by their more fortunate fellow inmates. People are to write, to think of one another, people are to give regards to those already gone: "If you run into Rika out there" . . . It is always out there, never Auschwitz, that word is never uttered. Out there. The vilest tempered, the crassest egotists become good Samaritans for a few hours. Then the procession lines up for the train; with all those knapsacks it is the lugubrious setting forth from a vagabond's conclave – our own *Beggar's Opera*. On the platform Schaufinger, with Bubi. Up to the last moment he remains accessible: couriers come in the nick of time from Amsterdam; he reads the petitions, most attentively, because he knows his duty; only Bubi sometimes distracts him, and then he may brush someone aside, as recently; when I started to go after him, he waved me away, calm personified. He stands at attention as the procession goes by him: *morituri eum salutant*. Let me confess it: he is better than we, we Jewish self-appointed VIPs. We, after all, cherish just one desire, that the train shall be off. That it shall be over with, that in our heated offices we may light the cigarette that we must not smoke here; we even feel a bit of resentment for the unfortunates in their cattle-trucks clinging to every moment they stay here, hoping for the miracle that never comes. And when the train finally rolls away, we go inside, as if from a funeral, numbed but relieved, with an irresistible craving for a cup of coffee, which we disparage even as we sit and drink it. And in the barracks the same quarrels again, now mostly over the distribution of the pitiful remnants of property left behind by the departed.

I HAVE ONLY a little time left. Again someone has come into the building whom I used to know, if only in passing: the young wife of a colleague from the former world of the High School. High pressure means quick cooking in physics as in human relations: we promptly call each other Dé and Jacques in the familiar fashion, as if it were the only natural way. Dé was taken in the train between Amersfoort and Lunteren during a check of identification papers. She is resigned, she is very brave, but still much worried about her husband: if only he doesn't get caught through her fault. While she sews a button on my coat, I talk to encourage her. She must need it, with all her pluck; I can feel it: "Citizen Evrémonde, may I hold your hand presently, when we ride to the guillotine?" A strange excursion, from Lamartine and Carlyle to Dickens – have I come no further than that?

It is now almost three weeks since I made my first attempt to write. This was after what Jacob has since called the Night of Herod, the night of the orphan children. A Flaubert of our day at least need not go back to Carthage to describe a slaughter of the inno-cents, except that Frau Wirth is not much like Salammbô. Perhaps the most gruesome part of all was the contrast between the children, who lay peacefully sleeping that night, and their attendants, who ran hither and thither like lunatics, trying to get one or two of the hundreds "embargoed". At five o'clock they were awakened for the journey to the slaughterhouse. They were, as I have said, orphan children, seized in a single "lightning raid" in the country; orphan children; yes, Jacob, I put the words down again, without comment; they speak for themselves. Some tried to hide, but on orders from Cohn the Disposition Service traced them down. Not all. Jacob, Jacob. Did I actually see the little girl lying under the bunk, or was it imagination? At any rate Rosa missed little Esther at the train, and Schaufinger had her replaced by another, an embargoed child; lucky that he was still in the same equable temper as always, because the wife of one of our constables took the preposterous and mortally dangerous liberty of pleading with him for "those poor little orphans"; she was a fairly crude and robust type, capable of saying something foolish at any moment, and I held my breath. "But the Führer has had orphanages built at Auschwitz," he reassured her with gentle reproach. "I'll show you the latest photograph of the Führer, talking so nicely with a couple of little girls; he's a great lover of children, you ought to know that." We all breathed easier at this long apostrophe, because on a previous occasion, when a non-Jewish woman I did not know had dared to plead for a shipment of children, he had sent her along, equipped with a star: "These children can never have too much company."

This time the company was pretty scarce, a number of punitive cases and a group of epileptics; the children were out of luck. Then, to the general astonishment, Sonja Ptaznik suddenly appeared from the corner; she was the daughter of a medical specialist, I think somewhere in Gelderland, and had gone to the bad. She had sunk so low (that is how they put it), and also grown so cynical, that she had simply put up over her bunk the sign from her father's office, "By Appointment Only". Cohn had characteristically dubbed her "the Hormonium", and had put her down for a previous train; on that occasion she had calmly mended runs in her stockings, and, having been fetched off the train in the very nick of time, heaven knows by whose intervention, she had resumed her old way of life. Sonja was for anybody who paid, much or little. Sonja was the most abject slut of the camp, which in these matters, as in others, had about it more of Gomorrah than I would have dared to dream in the days when women to me were named, perhaps not Beatrice, but at least Ninon. Sonja Ptaznik, the camp slut, you too a little Jewish sister of mine, you, Sonja, did what no one else that night could bring himself to, you gave yourself up of your own accord to go with those completely forsaken creatures. And you alone, Jacob, know how profoundly I was ashamed, I who had done nothing more than look at a bundle of clothes under a bench and dismiss it as a bundle of clothes, even though for a moment it seemed to move in the half-darkness.

The first time I did not get anything like this far, and the second time it went just as wrong, incidentally after a perfectly ordinary, relatively calm train night. At least it was scarcely unusual that someone, a woman, took her own life; it was actually an old acquaintance of mine, Miss Wolfson from the High School, who had once declared in the teachers' room at school, with the solemnity of an oath, that she would never leave Holland, and had kept her word. This last had not been so difficult, because in the city you can sometimes get cyanide more easily than vegetables, which are for sale to us only from three to five o'clock. At least I remember very well how just before I moved here I ran into Sam Wolfson, the only other Jew in my student debating club, and, having time to spare, how I went with him as he wanted to show me something special. And so it was, at least in a sense, because in the improvised home laboratory he maintained as an undergraduate medical student he had packed two pounds of the poison ("borrowed from an obliging chemist") in five hundred 2-gramme doses in little airtight tubes, of which he immediately offered me half a dozen, for my own use and for possible prospects.

Then he added a potted lecture: "Mind what I say, Jacques, because you're only an ignorant arts man – excuse the tautology. This stuff is called potassium cyanide. Don't nod your head – what do you know about it, you should live so long? It's a nerve stuff that any handbook will tell you about – it attaches itself to the haemoglobin of the red blood corpuscles, and then they won't absorb any more oxygen. Get it?"

"Certainly," I replied.

"Certainly," he mocked. "Well, that isn't the first

lie you've ever been caught in. Anyhow, take warning: eat these goodies and you're finished. Two grammes seems to me like plenty, but never mind. And here are a couple more. For all the *goyim* to butter their bread with after the war. The whole lot of them! Amen!" Because Sam was pretty fierce, and hated Protestants and Catholics alike.

Miss Wolfson, an aunt of his, I believe, also had one of these capsules with her; she had always carried it with her "for safety's sake", even at school during the algebra lesson; then she had only to open her handbag and peer into it, and she was reassured, she said; it gave her the splendid feeling that they couldn't do anything to her. She talked quite calmly about it that night; she was particularly intrigued by the fact that she had had to keep it dry, and now had to take it with water. Toward morning, with me accompanying her at her request, she went impassively to sit on her plank bed, and beckoned me close with an impassive, no, an almost bland expression: "Mr Henriques, will you promise me one thing?" I nodded. "Absolutely?" "Absolutely." "Good" (still levelly though tonelessly), "if anyone ever comes here named Karli Frenkel, Frenkel with an e, Dr Karli Frenkel, he's in his fifties and has gone underground, but if he ever comes here, you keep an eye on him." I gave her my hand silently; neither she nor I could help it if this smacked of pulp-fiction: I could hardly expect Miss Wolfson, the algebra teacher, to have me sacrifice a cock to Aesculapius. She said not another word, but firmly bit through the capsule and took a pull at the mug. She immediately clutched at her throat (apparently it was very painful), had violent cramps, gasped for breath, and turned ghastly pale; very shortly she was unconscious. A few more spasms, a bit of kicking and twitching, and she lay still. Georg's prediction had been right again: no tutoring from Miss Wolfson, in exchange for Black Market bread coupons. But she had not left Holland, and there she in turn had been right. And neither one of them had foreseen that I would be the one to close her eyes. In her stead, of course, someone else went aboard the train. To make up the number.

I offered Dé one of my capsules, but she refused, saying something so commonplace that it somehow moved me: "It's always five minutes too soon." It moved me, because she, like her husband, still bore on her wrists the scars of an abortive suicide attempt in 1940. I'll keep my supply for a while, anyway.

Thus far the night was normal enough, but at the train we had a small sensation after all. Not only did it happen that Schwarz, the second Service supervisor, was on staff duty that morning, but as I live and breathe Lizzy Heine came marching up. I had often seen the two strolling together, he a regular dandy with his light-gray trousers, check jacket, and bow tie, she with her fur cape nonchalantly draped around her shoulders, Deauville fashion. And now she appeared, impeccably turned out, as if for a festive occasion. Afterward I learned that in spite of Schwarz's supplications, trusting in her credit with Schaufinger, she had permitted herself this transgression of one of the most fundamental camp rules: no unauthorized persons on the departure platform. But she had wanted to experience this sensation: Westerbork bored her. I could not believe my eyes, and even Cohn, no friend of Schwarz's or hers, seemed thunderstruck. The drama took place in a couple of minutes, and I will try to record it as a monologue by Schaufinger; that at least is how I remember it: "Well, you here, Fräulein Heine! You have no idea how welcome you are. Most heartily!" She smiled, flattered, but Schwarz, quicker-witted than she, was already white as a sheet. "And how did you come here? Who invited you? You realize, of course . . . Oh, Herr Schwarz? Indeed, indeed. Herr Schwarz denies it? Well, that's odd, I must say. Please let's not have any wrangling here. Quiet, quiet, if you please! Once again, do you hear me, *quiet!* And do tell me, why did you choose to come here so early in the morning, of all things? You should have been resting for our cabaret, you know. Oh, you wanted to come and take a look? Yes, I can understand that; 'plunge both hands into the fullness of human life,' right? You needn't apologize, not at all, not at all." He smiled tenderly. "But here you only see the half of it; you should have a look at the whole thing, at the whole thing. *If* you please." I still don't know how he did it, but he seized her by the wrist, and as she, completely taken aback, offered no resistance, he pushed her into a truck. "And Herr Schwarz, may I invite you also . . . ?" Him Schaufinger did not even need to touch, for he followed her with bowed head; I caught one more glimpse of his bow tie below his open collar. "The young lady will also be able to sing in Auschwitz, no doubt," said Schaufinger, turning to us, as the train started to move. "A voice like a nightingale, like a nightingale, I tell you." Cohn nodded silently, for he was profoundly shocked – not about Schwarz, naturally, but about Cohn. Number two in the hierarchy, the crown prince of Westerbork, fallen like Icarus: the writing on the wall. "Oh, Suasso," he sighed on the way to our office, "is this damned war never going to be over?" He was absolutely impossible all day.

AND THE THIRD NIGHT, the night of my own downfall? It was even less sensational than the one before, though I was personally more involved. Without Hirsch it would never have happened, that much is sure. I had known the whole week that the "Rabbi" and his family would be going, because his list – and even he, poor fellow, was on a "protected" list – had come unstuck at The Hague. I knew it, and so did he. Of course I made an effort on his behalf with Cohn, but Cohn proved completely intractable. He began chaffing me a bit, and asked me how I had enjoyed Leah, the plucky little Jewish mama who was in Hut 16 with the twins. And when I indignantly denied this, he inquired if "that Mr Hirsch" had talked to me about the Pharisees in his "catechism" (naturally someone had told on us), and then preached me a little sermon not unlike the one at our first meeting, on the familiar subjects of hardness, blind obedience, and a bit more emphasis on the danger that threatened me if I did not obey his commands. Then he informed me that according to rumour the "Rabbi" and the Jews in the next transport were not to go to Auschwitz, but to a camp with some name like Sobibor, which nobody knew the truth about, but which must be some sort of "extermination camp", though not a soul knew the nature or method of the extermination. Even he could tell me no more, and I inclined – as I still do – to regard the whole affair as idle chatter and intimidation: if the Germans want to exterminate us, why not here? Why are they using an enormous mass of people and equipment for these trains when they so desperately need every soldier and every car? Think that over, says Jacob.

In any event, Cohn did nothing. That night, a week ago today, I had to read out the list in Hut 57, and he was on it: Jeremiah Hirsch, born March 16, 1910 – so he had just turned thirty-three. I called out his name, and from the abyss of silence one word came back: *"Hinneni"* – "here I am," as I now know. That was his reply from *Genesis*, from the depths. I helped him pack his knapsack; he consoled me. Jeremiah, my friend, my brother. In the early morning the routine procedure: the procession to the train. And he in the midst of it, with his Leah and his children, a boy and a girl of perhaps seven, among many parents and many children. He walked painfully; he was limping, and the knapsack was heavy; perhaps there were more books in it than usual, although he held in his hand the little black book I had so often seen him with: after all, a knapsack might get lost. On the platform he stumbled and dropped the book; he stooped with the greatest difficulty (that blessed knapsack!) to pick it up, but Cohn got there first, kicked it away, and hustled him roughly toward the truck; during a brief exchange of words that I did not catch Cohn finally gave him a bloody nose, while Schaufinger looked on, laughing. And then it happened, faster than I can tell it: I rushed at Cohn, struck him in the face with all my strength, picked up the book, and handed it back to the "Rabbi". As he stood in the door of the train, I can still feel the way he put his hands for a moment on my head, muttering a few words that I did not then understand, but now do grasp. And only then did the loud laughter of Schaufinger reach me, and he stood slapping his thighs: "Well, Cohn, so you're nothing more than a little Yid!" Cohn, pale as a corpse, beside himself with fury, roared something to a couple of Disposition Service men, who a moment later were driving me with kicks and blows to this building. Possibly it's my blood on my jacket, but I don't think so. That is all, everything, I have added nothing and left nothing out; that is all; this is what I have done, or what was done through me and with me: everything.

AND SO I HAVE FINISHED after all. Dé was even able to read it before it was smuggled out of the barracks. The sum has been added up, and there is an answer, right or wrong.

She sat for a long time staring straight ahead. Finally she came over to me and stroked my hair.

"Well, Dé? Say something, do!"

She smiled. "Tomorrow, when we're in the train. I've got to digest it all, and there are so terribly many questions. For instance, why did you hit Cohn and not Schaufinger? No, don't try now; tomorrow, in the train. In the train to Sobibor. Whatever happens, from now on I give you back your own first name, Jacob."

Harvill Paperbacks are published by Harvill,
an Imprint of HarperCollins publishers